D0996940

Can you spot the spider?

For Sharon (mew)

by Michael Broad

First published in 2007
by Hodder Children's Books

Text and illustration copyright © Michael Broad 2007

Hodder Children's Books
338 Euston Road
London NW1 3BH

Hodder Children's Books Australia
Level 17/207 Kent Street
Sydney, NSW 2000

The right of Michael Broad to be identified as the author and the illustrator of this Work has been asserted by him in accordance with the Copyright, Designs and Patents Act 1988.

All rights reserved

A catalogue record of this book is available from the British Library.

ISBN: 978 0 340 91778 7
10 9 8 7 6 5 4 3 2 1

Printed in China

Hodder Children's Books is a division of Hachette Children's Books.
An Hachette Livre UK Company

**MORAY COUNCIL
LIBRARIES &
INFO.SERVICES**

20 24 17 07

Askews	
JA	

SCAREDY CAT AND BOO

Michael Broad

Hodder
Children's
Books

A division of Hachette Children's Books

Scaredy Cat was scared.

He didn't like being home alone.
The floorboards creaking made him

shiver...

The sight of his shadow made him

quiver...

And the dark corners were dreadfully
dark and ever so

scary.

Scaredy Cat tried purring a cheery song
to sing away the scariness –

but it didn't work. He could still hear noises
everywhere. Mostly, there was a moaning,
sometimes a groaning, and this was always
followed by a loud...

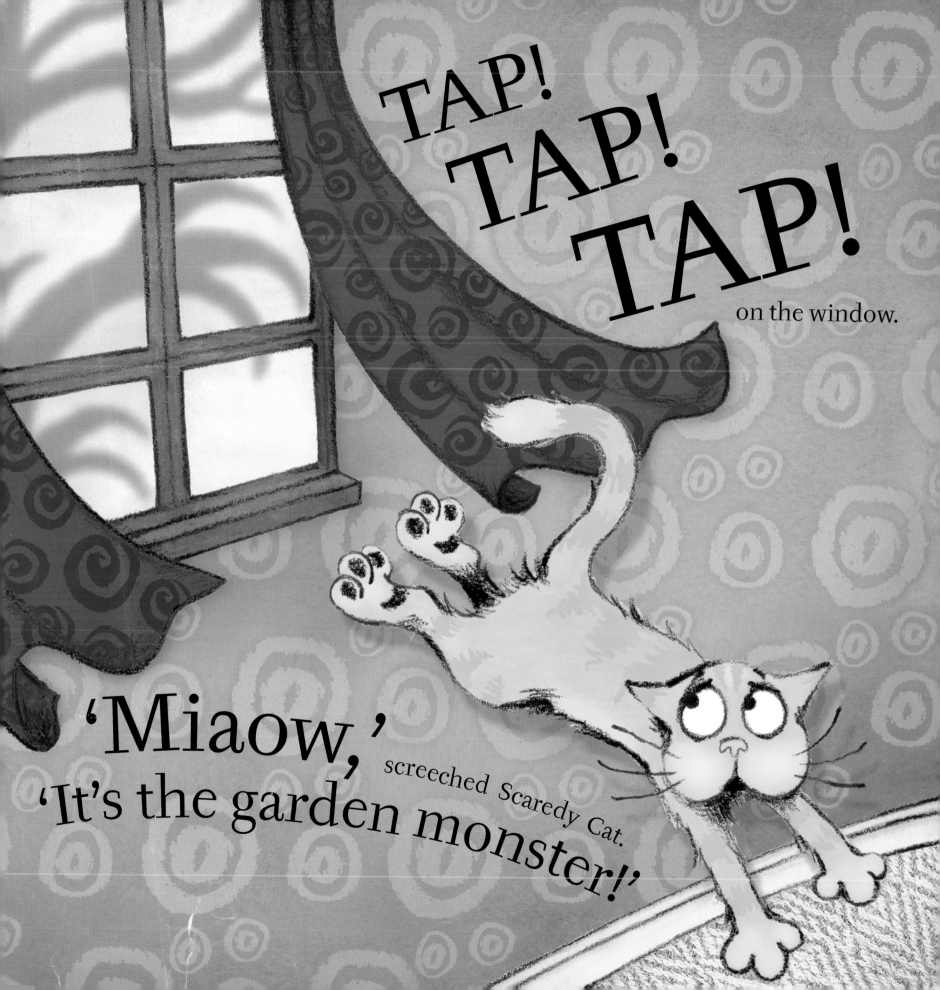

He ran to the laundry room to hide, but it was TOO dark.

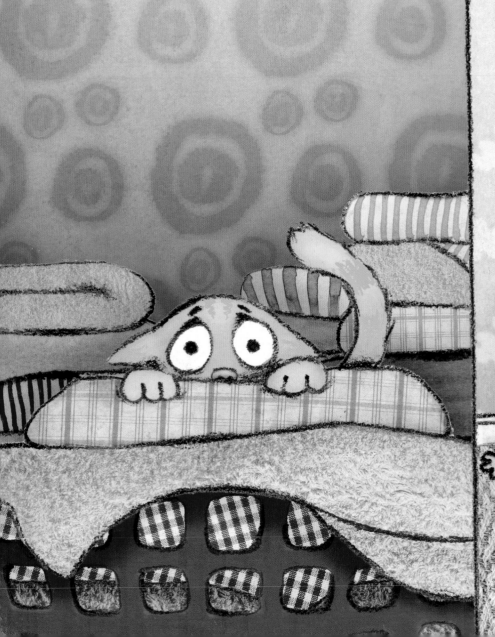

He ran to the bedroom, but it was full of strange creatures.

Finally, he tried
the bathroom.
DEFINITELY
no good!

'Miaow,' Scaredy Cat whimpered
and ran back to his basket,
where he hid beneath the soft,
warm and woolly blanket.
'Much better,' he thought,
WHEN...

'BOO!'
said a squeaky
voice beside him.

Scaredy Cat looked down from the ceiling
and saw a little mouse smiling up.
'I'm Boo!' said the mouse cheerily.
'Do you want to come outside and play?'
'N-no th-thank you,' stammered Scaredy Cat.
'There's a MONSTER outside!'

'I play in the garden and I've
never seen a monster,'
said Boo, laughing. 'Show me.'

So with chattering teeth,
Scaredy Cat led Boo to where
the MONSTER shadow loomed.
It was moaning and groaning
and going TAP!

TAP!

TAP!

on the window.

'That's not a monster,'
smiled Boo, lifting the
cat flap and jumping into
the garden. 'It's a tree for
climbing and for sitting
under when it's hot.
Trees are great.'

Scaredy Cat peered into the garden and saw
that the big thing with lots of arms didn't
really look like a monster anymore.
In fact, now he could see it properly, it looked like
something he would very much like to climb.

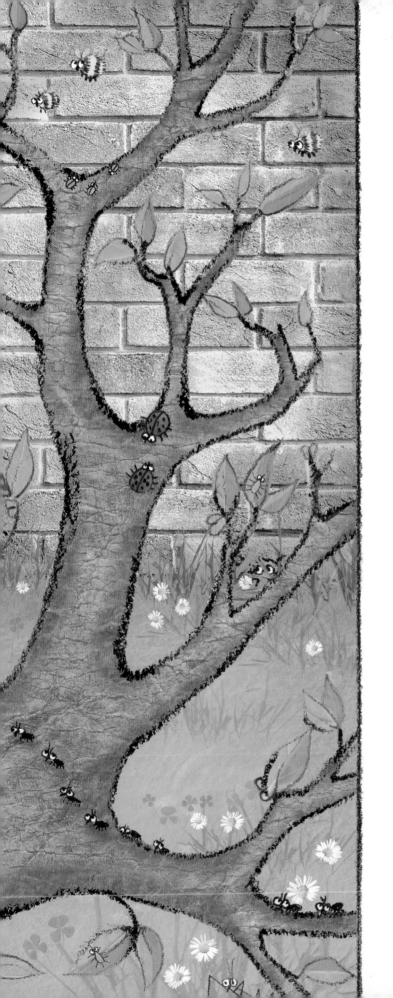

He looked at Boo smiling
and waiting outside the cat flap.
He took a deep breath, closed his eyes
as tight as they would go and placed one
trembling paw outside,

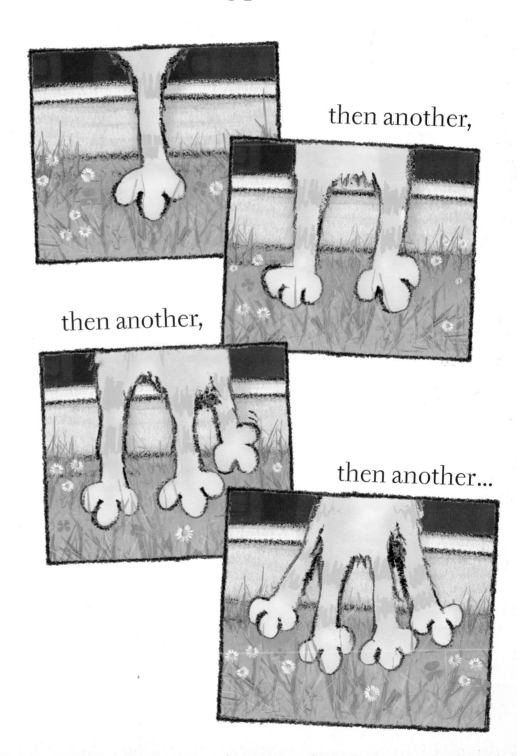

then another,

then another,

then another...

Scaredy Cat was outside!
He opened his eyes and
looked around.

The garden was wonderful.

But before Scaredy Cat could
take it all in, a butterfly landed
on his nose.

'I'm being attacked,' he whimpered,
waving his paws in the air.

'It's a butterfly,' explained Boo.
'They won't hurt you and they're
fun to chase.'

Then a sparrow swooped down and
landed on Scaredy Cat's head.

'HELP,' yelped Scaredy Cat,
hugging his tail for comfort.
'That's a bird,' said Boo.
'They sing funny songs.'

Scaredy Cat stepped backwards as the sparrow
flew off – and fell into a flowerbed.

'Come on,' Boo giggled, 'it's quite safe!
And it's time to go and play.'
Scaredy Cat looked at Boo and,
at last, he giggled too.

Scaredy Cat and Boo played hide-and-seek in the flowerbeds.

Then they chased butterflies and danced along to funny birdsong.

They even climbed the
MONSTER TREE, which was
the most fun of all because it was
a little bit SCARY...

Scaredy discovered he could be quite a
BRAVE CAT when he put his mind to it.

And BRAVE little Scaredy Cat could even scare his best friend...
BOO!